First published 2022
by Rowanvale Books Ltd
The Gate
Keppoch Street
Roath
Cardiff
CF24 3JW
www.rowanvalebooks.com
Library Cataloguing in Publication Data.
A catalogue record for this book is available from the British Library.

To my wife Adrianne, the diamond in my life,
and my wonderful family: Ian, Tina, Freya, Ayla and Osian.

Trevor the Tractor worked hard every day

And during the summer he gathered the hay

But summer was over and lying all round

Was a layer of snow all over the ground

The farmer's alarm
rang well before dawn

He left his warm bed
and gave a great yawn

He looked through the window and groaned with despair

When he saw how thickly the snow lay out there

He must rescue his animals before the next night
And get them to safety as quick as he might

He must also find someone to help with this task
And Trevor the Tractor was the best one to ask

Trevor was still fast asleep in his stall
When the farmer rushed in and gave him a call

He started his engine and roared into life
To help all the animals out of their strife

Shifting the snow, he found very hard

But he soon made a pathway across the farmyard

The pond was hard-frozen so he led the ducks back
Into the barn with many a quack!

The meadow was heaped up with snow that had drifted
But Trevor ploughed in and soon got it shifted

Quack!

Then the cows followed Trevor in ones and in twos
As they entered the barn, they thanked him with moos!

The chicken shed roof had just fallen in

Cluck!
Cluck!
Cluck!

And the chickens were running around in a spin

Cluck!

Cluck!

Cluck!

But Trevor drove in to save them – what pluck!

And the chickens all thanked him with cluck after cluck!

Neigh!

Neigh!

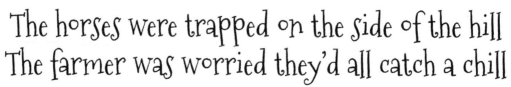

The horses were trapped on the side of the hill
The farmer was worried they'd all catch a chill

But Trevor plunged in and helped clear the way
And the horses escaped with a snort and a neigh!

The sheep were all trapped in a faraway field
The gateway was blocked and totally sealed

But Trevor in no time had the gate forced ajar
The sheep followed him back to the barn with a baa!

Baa!

But one little lamb was missing and lost

He was in great danger from naughty Jack Frost

But good old Trevor was clever and swift
He rescued that lamb from a huge snowy drift

Trevor the Tractor worked hard every day
There was never much time for Trevor to play

And even when temperatures dropped down to zero
He rescued the animals and was hailed as a hero!

Author Profile

John Davies was born into a mining family in the village of Cwmafan near Port Talbot in 1948. He attended Glanafan Grammar School and worked for thirty years as a chemist with BP Chemicals at Baglan Bay. He has been happily married to Adrianne for fifty years, and they have one son, Ian, who is happily married to Tina. Since retiring, John has pursued his hobbies of music, athletics and literature. He has played guitar in several bands and is currently a life member and president of Port Talbot Harriers.

John started writing for children when his first grandchild, Freya, was born. He now has two more grandchildren, Ayla and Osian, and has decided to continue writing in this genre because it suits his childish nature!

What Did You Think of Trevor the Tractor to the Rescue?

A big thank you for purchasing this book. It means a lot that you chose this book specifically from such a wide range on offer. I do hope you enjoyed it.

Book reviews are incredibly important for an author. All feedback helps them improve their writing for future projects and for developing this edition. If you are able to spare a few minutes to post a review on Amazon, that would be much appreciated.

Publisher Information

Rowanvale Books provides publishing services to independent authors, writers and poets all over the globe. We deliver a personal, honest and efficient service that allows authors to see their work published, while remaining in control of the process and retaining their creativity. By making publishing services available to authors in a cost-effective and ethical way, we at Rowanvale Books hope to ensure that the local, national and international community benefits from a steady stream of good quality literature.

For more information about us, our authors or our publications, please get in touch.

www.rowanvalebooks.com

info@rowanvalebooks.com

CPSIA information can be obtained
at www.ICGtesting.com
Printed in the USA
LVHW070411120722
723217LV00002B/12